Twilight Light (The Second Volume)

Gopal Patra

ISBN 978-93-5610-733-5
© Gopal Patra 2022
Published in India 2022 by Pencil

A brand of

One Point Six Technologies Pvt. Ltd.
123, Building J2, Shram Seva Premises,
Wadala Truck Terminal, Wadala (E)
Mumbai 400037, Maharashtra, INDIA
E connect@thepencilapp.com
W www.thepencilapp.com

Author biography

Author Biography
Gopal Patra: - The life of a poet-storyteller is an invincible soldier who fought in battle - whose tool is fearlessness and honesty ... Search Google for details and type in Bengali or English letters. If you search "Gopal Patra" you will get all the information!

Address :-Gopal Patra
Vill- Bhagabati Pur
P.O - Chaturvuj kati
P.S - Shankrail
Dist- Howrah
Pin Cod - 711313
West Bengal - India
Mobile number:- 9143098660

Email address:-patragopal561@gmail.com
Facebook link:-
https://www.facebook.com/profile.php?

CONTENTS

Twilight Light (The Second Volume)

Twilight Light
(The Second Volume)
A sweet love story
Gopal Patra

Dedication: - First love

Twilight Light

Volume II

After finding each other and exchanging various memories of their youth, Mau and Sajal meet each other in private and express their happiness and sorrow.

And Mauu found his first love Sajal and went to his mother's temple in Kalighat and worshiped together!

At the mother's temple, Sajal Mau wanted to give some presents, so Mau requested Sajal to buy a box of vermilion and a pair of branches and leaves. Sajal Ke got a decent job and Mauu published a book of Sajal from Ananda Prakashani on his own initiative.

In return, Sajal Mauu wants to know what he wants. Mouu says if Digha or Puri beach wants to spend one day and one night in solitude with him then it will happen! Is there any danger in going to Digha? Or the flow of life will begin a new.

Author Biography

Gopal Patra: - The life of a poet-storyteller is an invincible soldier who fought in battle - whose tool is fearlessness and honesty ... Search Google for details and type in Bengali or English letters. If you search "Gopal Patra" you will get all the information!

Address :- Gopal Patra
Vill- Bhagabati Pur
P.O - Chaturvuj kati
P.S - Shankrail
Dist- Howrah
Pin Cod - 711313
West Bengal -
Mobile number- 9143098660

Email address:- patragopal561@gmail.com

Facebook link:-
https://www.facebook.com/profile.php?

Table of contents

Chapter Twelve

Ithought I would end the love story of Sajal and Mau here ...

And not a face-to-face meeting that will happen via messenger ... Mouu's passion - crying in front of people at the Victoria Gate ... Twenty-one years later, hiding the face of the old lover's chest with pride!
Cooking the terms I like ... is beyond imagination - And in the mother's temple in Kalighat, the mental ..

And I begged you to buy me something - a bundle of vermilion and a pair of shells - the urge to buy something ...
Isn't that unusual?

I did not understand so much because I have not spent a single penny of my gate since the morning of the eighth day! Maui did all the expenses! That's why I said- But the result is the opposite ...

However, I bought it without any objection - Mauu Shankha said with a blush on his forehead - How long have I fulfilled my desire - And he said that from today onwards I am yours again Sajal.

After saying goodbye to Mauu on the evening of Ashtami, I could not reconcile those manners ...

The size of the container is whatever the girls or the water container is kept in ...

That's why after getting married, why does the lover forget about his relatives and even his parents! But is Mau the exception?
Couldn't change shape? But why?

Mouu has no misgivings? How many stories of fame are being published in various social media and print media!

I will not be stuck somewhere in any way? I am a young man - what will happen to them when four stomachs revolve around me?
Although the day was not quite comfortable - there was no lack of love - affection - love - friendship! Go ahead or go back? There are so many types it's hard to say. Honestly, Mauu has not been contacted on Messenger since that day with such thoughts ... Besides, Pujo spent a lot of time with his children and family ...

But this morning I saw Mauu's message I turned on the messenger ... I was shocked when I saw the message ...

In a few days, Mauu has uprooted a mountain of thousands of words.
Wishing you a happy victory, he sent me a few pictures of the game of Cinnamon. And he said that after

so many years he has enjoyed such a pleasure in the game of Sindur or is it just for me! Complaint or forget your mauu? And how many self-written verses full of pain and pain - the bleeding of pain after wearing it.

The first offer is that she has got a respectable job for me with her husband and political grandfather!

I would like to contact the Bidhannagar Municipality by eleven next Monday at the next fourteenth date - and Mauu will be there in person!

Mauu also said that you think the job of political grandparents? Does that mean party-slaves ... the party in power has to be enslaved? But it's not ... You believe me, come on, but ... don't miss it ...

Another big surprise is waiting for you but I'll tell you - not now ....

****

Chapter Thirteen

Whatdo I do now? Our War House will open today ... After six or seven days of continuous vacation, the workload and vacation will not match!

Maybe after working for a while, I didn't like the work of the municipality ... or they didn't consider me worthy ...

The real thing is not being told openly to anyone else or to the housewife - because what if the opposite happens? With all these thoughts and thoughts, I have not been able to concentrate on my work at all.

After eating and drinking, I thought in my cold head, "Okay, let's not have a discussion with Mauu about that work ... What's the harm in that?"

Can anyone tell when life will turn in a direction like a flowing river? Let's not show .. Besides, my long time acquaintance Mauu will surely do something good for me!

With this in mind - having a cup of tea from work on Saturday - I caught Mau in the messenger ... Although the seven seas are not the names of the thirteen rivers, I tried to refute all the values and conceits of Mauu in the story of five seas and ten rivers.

Mouu seems to be a little annoyed and wrote the story of the seven seas and thirteen rivers ... Are you coming on Monday? Everything has to come ...

I didn't write it, I mean, what do you mean ... I told you first, believe me - you deserve what you deserve! Yeah Al that sounds pretty crap to me, Looks like BT aint for me either.

Without further ado, I just said .. I will come .. will you stay? Hey dad, I promised - I will stay - I will stay - I will stay. Remember not to be late - eleven ...

I spent the night floating on the shores of the river. On Sunday morning I went to the market for Lakshi Puja. As usual, I went to the market.

After hearing all this, Ginny said, "Well, don't try ... if anything happens!" I mumbled, but it would take four or five hours to get away! Ginny said what? If the work is honorable - and the recommendation is sure to happen ...

Let's leave Baba Hap ....
 OK, that's all there is to it .... Get ready tomorrow morning! How do I recover from the bath?

All right, everything will be ready - Ginny said!

Sunday was somehow cut short by anxiety ... I took a bath on Monday morning, dressed modestly and took the accompanying papers! Remembering Isht Dev ... I said goodbye to everyone in the house - I crossed the unknown path ...

****

Chapter Fourteen

FromSankrail station to Howrah station Howrah to Bidhan Nagar bus .... When I reached the municipality, it was exactly eleven o'clock in the morning!

I caught Mau on the phone - Hello Mau, where have you reached? Yes, Sajal, I am waiting for you at the main gate .... Come on!

When I reached the main gate, I was alone ... Mauu is not going to Chennai! That day was undressed but today it is absolutely gorgeous Fashionable .. Mauu has a lot of jewelry ...

Coming a little closer, he looked at me from side to side and said in a tone of excitement, "Very good boy ... the time has come!" He showed me a shiny double BM car in front of me and said that it was my car .. and that my driver Ramjivan ...

Ramjivan addressed me and said- Salam saheb ... I also greeted you politely!
The rest will be later. Now let's go to the mayor's house.

After opening the door, Mauu said, "Grandpa is coming ..." The mayor, seeing Mauu, folded his hands and said, "Mrs. Sen ... what a blessing for me ... sit down, sit down!" We both sat down ...

Mayor Collingbell Tippey came in immediately ... tell me sir .... The mayor said Mrs. Sen will eat tea or coffee? Whatever you say will be Dada - Mauu said ....! Let's make three coffees and see ... Sir ... the man said goodbye!

This is the civilized photo I told you about! And yes, what is the name brother? Ajne - Sajal Das I said!

OK brother, your job will be done! Dr. Sen says everything about you - wait a minute ....
Thank you sir I said!

The coffee arrived at the right time, we were sipping coffee ... and the mayor seemed to call and explain to me!

After drinking coffee, the mayor pressed the calling bell again and immediately a person came ... showed me and told me to take Anna to Ramesh Babu's house..say I sent-
All right? The man nodded in agreement!
The man addressed me and said come with me .... if I try to go -

Mauu immediately said - then come today grandfather? Doctor Babu who will greet my Vijay ... now he is not in Bangalore?
Yes Grandpa ... Mauu said ...

OK, when he returns, how can I go there and eat at Petpur one day?

He is my lucky grandfather. You go with him   I'm waiting in the car outside .... Mau said goodbye ...

I entered Ramesh Babu's cabin with the gentleman. The gentleman showed me and said that the mayor sent Anna ...

As soon as I sat in the chair, the gentleman said that there is no problem when you know the mayor - the work is nothing but assistant tax collected ...!

There are so many types it's hard to say. You will not have to be happy with all that! Please give me the bio data ... I gave the bio data ... He turned his eyes and said Excellent - Very good .... This is the kind of computer savvy we wanted!

Okay brother wait a minute I am getting the apartment letter ready .. So how do you join from tomorrow?

I said politely if Sir Salary would say that a little bit - he would say 21000 / - plus at the beginning .... also you will get ESIP-PF and other benefits!

Thank you very much sir ...

After a while he handed me the apartment letter and said how is the office tomorrow at eleven o'clock ... Room number 26. All right?

Thank you very much sir .... Coming sir ...
Come on ...

Ramesh wants to get out of Babu's cabin and go to Mauu in a hurry.
But where is Mauu? Yeah Al that sounds pretty crap to me, Looks like BT aint for me either.

I caught Mau on the phone - Hello, where are you?

Yeah Al that sounds pretty crap to me, Looks like BT aint for me either.   Yeah Al that sounds pretty crap to me, Looks like Al that sounds crap to me, Looks like Al that sounds crap to me, Looks like Al that sounds crap to me OK - OK - I hung up the phone ...! I started thinking about the recommendation Majesty ... The mayor thought it was Dr. Sen's man ... Ramesh Babu thought it was the mayor's man .... Everything was done with respect like magic ....

My heart sank with gratitude for Mauu ... I waited anxiously for him ....

Mouu's phone rang in ten minutes ... Please wait a minute, I have some leftovers to buy - How are I coming in five minutes ...

OK Mauu - Five minutes why am I willing to wait for you all my life ... because I know you are my best friend ...

Mauu smiled and said ... Is that so? All right, keep it up!

****

Chapter Fifteen

Aboutfive minutes later, Mauu's car pulled up in front of him. Come up He said softly ... Please come up ...

Somehow I got in the car and the two of us got in the back seat - the car started ...

Rabindra Sangeet was playing softly in the car. I don't know. Coincidentally, the next song ...

I lose every moment to find you anew He is the treasure of my love.   You are invisible to be seen, He is the treasure of my love. Ogo, you are not my secret, you are my forever--   Immerse yourself in the current of the momentary leela, He is the treasure of my love. I tremble with fear when I find you--   When I feel a wave of love. There is no end to you, so finish yourself off with zero,   That laughter washes away the tears of my separation, He is the treasure of my love.
 (Rabi Thakur)

Mouu leaned on my side, put his hands on my lap, gently put his head on my shoulder, and opened his eyes with emotion .... I started to understand Ravi Thakur's song ...

"Every now and then I lose you because I will find you anew He is the treasure of my love. "
Mou is hiding her face in my chest and sobbing ... My eyes are also listening ...
The whole body is trembling ... I understand the unspoken words are falling down in tears ... I hugged the two of them tightly - intensely!
I don't know ..
Whether Bidhata smiled invisibly !!!

The car got stuck at the traffic signal - The car stopped and the song stopped .... I restrained myself and asked only one question, where are we going Mauu?

In my flat - I mean, where do we live?

Maybe ... but come on, once you see my house, household ... and at least it will be a little sweeter ... you don't owe Vijaya sweets?

Do I just owe Mau? I have nothing to give? You have nothing to ask me?

You don't know how much you have given Sajal unknowingly ... You have given me back the old taste of life - I have woken up from the sleep of death and I am going again to fulfill my dream ...

Yeah Al that sounds pretty crap to me, Looks like BT aint for me either.

Mauu gently touched my chin and said ... he doesn't talk - please don't be angry ... Come with me - I will not delay you!

The good news of Jan Mau has not been announced at home yet!

Why Oma? Let me know now ...

Tell me everything? I mean car love ... Mouu smiled softly and said - if you have courage, let me know ....

Trying the phone -

Mauu is looking at me with a sweet smile on his face ...

Hello

Hello Dad ... (In little girl's voice)

What are you doing honey I'm just playing games ..

Where is mother?

Give it to mom?

Yes ...

Hello ...

Hello, you know I'm done ...

This is very good news, don't forget to invite that friend one day - such friendship is not found nowadays!

I must say yes ...

When will you return home - will it be too late to return?

I do not understand the new works, so it will be a little late!

Okay - talk to the girl ...

Give ....

Hello Dad ... is your job done? Then bring sweets?

Yeah Al that sounds pretty crap to me, Looks like BT aint for me either.

Yes I do ....

The car has started moving- is Ginny happy then Mouu said ..,

Yeah Al that sounds pretty crap to me, Looks like BT aint for me either.

He said friend, maybe .. girlfriend wouldn't let you come or not?

That's not all ... Life in the hometown is socialism - friends rarely understand ...

Husband-wife-son-daughter-in-law-mother-in-law ...

I was joking, Sajal - I understand everything ... It's a big hobby, I go and see your golden family with my own eyes ....

I also want you to go and see my reality with your own eyes ...

I will definitely go one day ....

Mem sub car parking lot - or garage? Parking lot ...

After a while Saheb will leave at Howrah station!

Yes ma'am ...

B-Block Lake Town - Sector Five - Flat Number Thirty One ... It is my address .... Welcome to my house .... Please come ...

Skyscraper - I am getting up in the elevator ... Once I arrived at flat number thirty one ...

Adequate light and air allowed me to sit in a drawing room. Mauo went in.

I am looking around like Handaram and wondering where Mauu is and where I am ..

After a while Mauu changed his clothes and sat down in my opposite chair with a plate full of sweets and water.

Then he smiled and took a message in his hand and said .. eat it and make it sweet then I will give the real news ...

I ate sweet tuku in Mauu's hand and I also fed Mauu a sweet in my own hand!

You know, Sajal, when you first came to my house, I couldn't feed you anything else! I was very tense about your work ... so I couldn't cook anything. Eat sweets wholeheartedly ...
If that luck ever happens then I will cook and feed you your favorite dish ... I promise.!
Bao ....! Will you cook and eat ...?

Yeah Al that sounds pretty crap to me, Looks like BT aint for me either.
Tell me, when will you take me home?
The day God gives ...
You'll be gone in a moment ... I don't know when I'll find you again Sajal.

I am alone in this sixteen hundred square foot flat .... Mr. Sen in an emergency meeting in Bangalore - boy hostel - girl went for a walk with girlfriends in Mandarmoni - the flat is coming to swallow me ... so he does not want to say goodbye ... let's leave everything and go out with you - will you take me with you Sajal?

I couldn't think of anything to say.

Besides, I will come to you from time to time when the office is closed! You will see me too ... and call when you feel very alone ...

Didn't you say I have nothing to ask of you? That's what I want from you ... that's why I dragged you so far I want to live on my own ...

Yeah Al that sounds pretty crap to me, Looks like Al that sounds pretty crap to me, Looks like Al that sounds pretty crap to me, Looks like Al that sounds pretty crap to me.

So let it be Sajal .. Look at how I lost my mood on this happy day ... Please eat some more sweets .... Surely you are very hungry?

Don't worry about it, I ate and went out - okay eating sweets ... But the time that flows through me ... to give the good news ... where to give it?

I'm dying - I forgot - OK, I'm coming ... You sit down ... That's like a good girl. I said excited!

After a while, Mauu came back with some packets in his hand ... At first he said - Here's your Pujo gift ... I said what's in it? Two sets of pants ...

I said what was the need Mauu?

Mister was needed - would you wear a shirt and pants to the office - I will not tolerate that .... you are our man now!

You mean, like, saltines and their ilk, eh? Don't understand?

You don't have to understand ...
    I mean nothing else .... our katta means Dr. Sen Mayor Sabhya Da who said you or his cousin ... what else!

I said jokingly ... and I am your brother now ... that means ...

    Mauu replied immediately after taking the word out of his mouth - yes the second groom - do you have the power? I'll try it later ... Now close your eyes and see -

I understand the eyes ....
He handed me a small packet ... I thought it would be a book ...

As I said before, there are two good news waiting for you ... It's not a lie, now open your eyes- And open the packet ....
I opened my eyes - Mou's face is bright with sweet smile ....
I opened the packet full of emotion - I can't believe my eyes!

I look at the Agapashtala book upside down, it is a book, but my book of poetry .... a. "Ek Chilte Roddur" published by Publishers.
    On the back of the hard-wrapped book, I saw a small picture and a short acquaintance of the poet! And the

cover has been covered with famous painting art!

How did all this happen? I asked a foolish question who is Mauu ...

Mouu said in a calm voice- I know you will not misunderstand me ... Some of your selected poems mean some poems that I like. Sends to the publisher's office! They like it and Sharad expressed his desire to publish it in numbers and requested to send some more writing ..! Then I e-mailed some poems from your profile and sent them to that department ...

Maybe you needed approval! But believe me, I'm going to give you a surprise - I'm sorry if I'm wrong!

Don't say that ... I am ready to endure such a mistake for the rest of my life ... But how much more will you do for me? Am I worthy of all this?

I am doing it for you because I am worthy - you will do everything according to your ability - I am just changing the path as a good friend ...
The job of a good friend is to elevate each other ... to complement each other!
I also believe in my heart ... But .... But again, why?

So much happiness will be sewn on our foreheads? You know what I dreamed last night ...

What dream ...?

You and I are going somewhere .... maybe in search of happiness - how many kinds of beautiful flowers are blooming all around .... Hand in hand - hand in hand ...
Suddenly there is no cloud - no rain, just water and water around the road ... watery ... They're both sinking ...

Mauu was a little upset when he heard the dream in my mouth but he immediately said please take this envelope.

I opened the envelope and saw a shelf check and noticed the amount was fifty thousand!
Why is that?
This is your first royalty ...
I have taken a self check by requesting Atanu Da as the spelling of your account number is unknown ....

It's unimaginable just surprise after surprise ....
Mauu began to say again- You must be thinking? How did you get acquainted with Atanu Dar? Before that. How many books have I published from the publisher ... will I give them to you at the right time for the right price? But not now ...

I thought to myself, that's why I was amazed when I read the first text of the messenger - how can there be such a nakshi kantha sister - my lost mau - sunshine in my chile room "
What do you think?

I think ... I am willing to give you everything, I have nothing to give you ... but how can we have two hands and feet tied! Look at how lonely ... I can't be two! We are like the inhabitants of another planet .. Suddenly our arrival is like a comet!

I am saying these words passionately when Mauu is cutting my hair with his head on his chest ... again I am saying ...
There's nothing you can do about it ...
Here you are in solitude, immersed in the pursuit like a solitary ascetic! Whose only companion is loneliness ... Ever bereaved woman!

I keep saying that Mauu is holding his head on his chest and Billy is cutting his hair and I am bathing in tears ...

On that day, with all the disbelief - with all the abandonment, my heart was filled with sweet emotion - I was saying goodbye to Mauu! All hearts and souls are full of gratitude!

****

Chapter Sixteen

Ihave joined a new job at the right time - I don't feel bad! Giving and receiving a certain amount of tax receipts and uploading all the data to the computer!

Meanwhile, regular messages are being exchanged with Mouou on Phone Messenger ... This is the day when suddenly Mouu sat down - will you pay me?

I said what do you want to say? I don't owe you anything ...

He said I want you a whole day and night!
That's the diameter?

I just want to make you my own one day .... I want to fulfill all the desires of life - tell me, will you give it to me?

Yes, I promised ... but how many more days do you understand? A new job can't be earned all of a sudden.

What's more ...
I also said that the heat of the sun picking oysters on the sand of the sea all day long is a little humid, which means a little cold and not let go for a few days. Moreover ...

And again?

Apart from that, other ancillary work is better in winter? What do you say Mauu?
And Hari is so much under you? OK so sign ...
It's like a golden girl ...

This is how many more days have passed - seeing the last Saturday of November, the time has been fixed!

Hotel Booking - All Programs Accessory
And me Mauu - of b. W. M Car will pick up my local area from Ranihati ....
OK full and final ..?

Yes sir ...

I have already said at home that I have to go out for office work one day .. so no one objected because new job - that kind of work!
No more barriers - I'm standing at the Ranihati bus stop at eight o'clock in the morning with as little luggage as I can ... but where is Mauu?

I tried on the phone for a while but the phone switched off .. what's the matter? Mauo doesn't usually do that .... Last night we talked too - no danger sign ... But what happened?

Seven or five different thoughts come to mind - half an hour passed like this ... then maybe seeing my serious condition - someone said from a distance - this is where I am ... I looked and saw Mau .. What are you calling so often? I haven't noticed a BWM car standing in the stand for so long!

I saw the car once so I couldn't figure out the number .... Besides, it was said that Mau would wrap me in the moving car - who knew he would arrive before eight!

I was embarrassed and said - what else but why did you keep the phone off?
Mauu laughed and said - to see how you are - so the sweet shop in front Waiting! Babu is in such a hurry to go?

All is well and I will not be late. Get in the car Hurry up ...

****

Chapter Seventeen

Assoon as he got up, the car started! Only Mau and I ... sat side by side - side by side - side by side!

I said will you see the driver?
Mouu laughed and said - Ramjiban has a long experience of driving a car - so he knows what Babu-Bibira does in the back ... so it is forbidden to see them even if you have a hundred wishes! You understand the eyes and quietly put your head on my chest and take a little rest! There's a lot of work to be done ...
I can do everything Mauu- you see I can do everything right!

Ok shut up now
BWM car is moving smoothly along Bombay Road ... I am dreaming with my head on my chest ... half-sleep-half-awake dreaming ... as if there is no harm in not breaking this sleep!
Mauu is singing to me ...

"Every now and then I lose you because I will find you anew He is the treasure of my love. "
Who knows where so much happiness was hidden when the lifeboat was in the middle of the sea?

Shelter is so safe that there is no fear or unknown fear ... The two of you who are intoxicated with the desire to fulfill all the desires of the heart - complement each other!
Only one leaf of the tree of life found close to the two of them - one day! So what or less?
After a while I tried to get up but I couldn't.
Now open your eyes, maharaja ... Why Empress? At the destination that appeared .... If this journey had been going on for eternity, it would have been better.

OK, Mister, we still have a whole day and a night in our hands! Now, please, please ...
In front of the hotel "Blue Moon" Mauu stood in front of the reception! Seeing the aristocratic look, the receptionist said - Madam, how can I help you? Our hotel was booked by Maumita Das Wife of Sajal Das ... Okay madam, please take a minute ... The receptionist said looking at the booking list Yes Mum Room Number 46- Please sign here- Mau signed ...

Take the waitress to room number 46 ... Yes sir- he took us and we followed him- little luggage so there was no problem in the book! Room number 46 came to see!
He opened the key of the waiter's gate and explained which bathroom, which dressing room, which AC, which fridge, which TV switch! Mau shook his head .... When we need to press this red button we will show up immediately ... All right, ma'am?
Mau agreed ...

****

Chapter Eighteen

Mouusaid wash your hands and face and come fresh - there is some puri and curry with it-- how can I go to the bath after eating and drinking?

When the meal was over, it was about quarter to twelve - Mauu came back from the dressing room after a while to get ready - I saw Mauu's dress and immediately told him ....

Mem Saheb - what else is like Subedar! What more can I say .... My little bermunda and jeans- Mouu looked at me from the back and said OK - that's it ...

It's not too late now ...

Anyway ....

We stood side by side on the beach for a while. The waves are rising and falling.

I said anxiously - "I am one of the weary souls - the sea of life around me - the wildness of Natore gave me peace! (Jibanananda Das)

Mouta Mita Sen of Laketown in my case!

I put my hand on Mouu's face and put my hand on his shoulder. Sweet smile on his face.

Mauu is like a mermaid- here and there, never disappear again- calling me by name ... as if I can't get any shore!

Ever wanted to grab me and swallow me wholeheartedly ... The sky is shaking with the laughter of Mauu!

Fear is running through my mind - the waves seem to smile near the big teeth! As if he is making fun of me!

Meanwhile Mauu is shouting - well you said - that you are all work What happened?
Even if I want to, I can't compete with Mau - I can't do it even if I lose ...

For the sake of the bee, I shouted, "Deep on the other side - come a little closer, please ..."
Why are you afraid Come on, if you don't save me, I will sink ...

I hugged Mau tightly ... Mau grabbed me with all his being and started absorbing all the rays of body and mind!

Both of them gave each other everything in earnest! It's been a while since I've had this ...
Mouu e said let's get up this time! I wanted that in my mind - but I said in my mouth right now?

So Mauu said - our time is short - I got you one day for one night ... to fulfill all the desires of life in this time?

Mau all the desires are fulfilled in life?

I know Sajal, but I found you like a lost dream - I enjoy it as much as I can! The atmosphere seemed so heavy that I didn't talk anymore .. I put my hand on Mauu's shoulder and pulled him close and gently kissed him on the forehead!

I said- so let's get up!
Both of them are starving after doing enough exercise in the sea .... so without any delay I changed my clothes and came down to the hotel for a meal and sat face to face in a secluded seat!

The waiter brings up the menu list ....
    Mou liked it all - but showed me once before ordering - I rolled my eyes ...

White rice Mug dal - Vegetables- Sukta - Eggplant fried- Fry Rice- Chicken tan- Hilsa fish pot- Shrimp Malaikari- Pabda Fish Salt - Tapse Fish Chop - Mango Chutney Saka Papar - Yogurt - And big rasgolla -
Okay, perfect ... I said!

The waiter is arranging all the terms one by one - it's as if I'm dead! I remembered the house very much - especially my six year old little girl - my housewife ...

And no doubt, they worship me like a distant deity - in such a royal way AC car - AC hotel room - such royal food has never been eaten together ...

I've been here two or three times before - but what about ordinary middle-class people, family rooms of five to seven hundred rupees - ordering some good and bad food at a bargain price ...

Then at the end of the month I have to eat boiled pulses, rice and potatoes for a few days!

Seeing me a little upset, Mouu said- do you remember the house-housewife?

How do you know

I understand everything Sajal - I am a housewife - a mother ... but the bonds of my kinship have almost come loose after a long time! But you are bound by that hard bond ... This is normal for you -

For me - I have come so far only to give priority to my desires ... I do not understand - or I do not know ... I was saying please - one day the book is nothing!

Please start eating - otherwise the whole responsibility will fall on me!

I was going to say something to comfort Mauu ... He said with a sigh - OK, start eating first! Please talk later! I said- that Anje Maharani ...

The line of laughter on the lips of Mauu! I am eating with complete satisfaction ... Mauu is giving me half of most of the food ... before eating!

You know, Sajal, I don't eat much - you eat too much ... I understand - Mauu, but he is not showing me mercy!

As the wife - for the beloved man   gives everything she owns - deprives - deprives herself ... so ......

After a moment of silence, Mauu opened his mouth for the first time - this time, if we ever have to come, we will all come together!
What does that mean? I asked the question.
Everyone thinks my family if anyone comes And everyone in your family! Is that possible? I asked ...

It is possible to introduce me to your accountant - I will make such an impression ... You will see that I will send you by force even if you do not want to!
So that is Mauu!

You just have to be more discriminating with the help you render toward other people.
You can become a millionaire in the new year in the chair you are sitting in! But in a dishonest way - I don't know what you will do! You can't! You don't have to! I'm arranging for two or three of your books to be published in the next issue of Book Fair! See if your monthly income is at least one thousand and fifty!

And I will try to arrange for a flat next to our building to be given to you in installments! Then you and I are all members of your family Together!

The dream did not become a little sky-sky - is it possible in reality?

Everything is possible, just try, I am here!
Did you know that Mauo never had any ambition because maybe someone like you didn't dream ...

On the way to the end of the meal, seeing the leaves empty, Mauu said, "Shall I boil a hilsa?" No, believe me, this time my stomach will probably burst .. so much food
I played for the first time in my life! Shall I say something?

Why do you hesitate to tell me-
I said at least let me pay the lunch bill?
And this - give it then ...
I went to the reception and paid the bill of 34 show money - we both went upstairs ....
****

Chapter Nineteen

Wet the door and turn on the AC in normal mode. ....

I came to my bed with a haughty face and lay down ...

Mouu said in silence for a while - is the gentleman angry or not? I don't mean ... I mean nothing ... lie back to me - just look at each other - and yes, my eyes are always open but ... I got a big smile in my mind - !
That like a good boy - Mau said ...

There is no sleep in each other's eyes. What kind of resonance is going on in the mind but it cannot be expressed in words, yet I said - how can it not seem like a dream Mauu?

Yes, the dream is over tonight, there will be nothing! Why not, everything will be in the mind room - I said!

Now let's take a short walk in the sajal dune then in the middle of the dune pile - put your head on my lap and watch the sunset for a while!

Well, Mauo can be the opposite? I mean, you can't put your head on my chest!   Maybe, but it's out of order. From the time of that "Adam-Eve" till today, women have been the shadow companions of men - companions - shadows "

But if all men obeyed that - if the evaluation of women was correct then the condition of society would not be like this today!

He said the words with a big arrogant face ... Mauu is speaking the truth. I went silent!
Mou is ready to dress up - I too ...

Walking side by side in the sand, I can see the various achievements of different people. Getting a smile sometimes! I've come a long way, so I said let's sit here and go back?
Mau signed my words!

There is a little bit of sunshine but not much energy - like old age .....

In the sand dunes, Mauo's head is no longer in his lap. There is not much environment, moreover, the gathering of people is wide... necessarily the two of us sat side by side!
The sky and the sea are one and the same - like Mau and my heart, mind and soul -

The sun is changing color little by little! The sound of the sea roaring - the wind is blowing with the sound of thunder ব some migratory birds are flying towards the destination by the side of the red sun like the yolk of an egg - after a while the sun turned red like the tip of a vermilion!

Thousands of birds are returning to their nests.

Come on Sajal, the day is over for us - I said the night is still left!

As soon as he returned to the room, the calling bell rang and a waiter appeared. Tell me, madam? Now a cup of coffee - Anything else? Nothing more now!

I said what will you eat at night madam?

Bread - vegetables ... A glass of fruit juice and a glass of hot milk ...

Yes ma'am ...

Yeah Al that sounds pretty crap to me, Looks like BT aint for me either.

Okay madam so be it ...

The waiter went back and after a while went for a cup of coffee!

Mouu switched on the TV while sipping a cup of coffee - it was almost eight o'clock while searching for some favorite channel!

Then there was a knock on the door.

It was eight o'clock when the TV switched off. Mouu said let's start eating and drinking - I started eating curry - bread and some kind of vegetables! Hand-made bread tasted good - I finished eating!

Sit still. Mauu grabbed one of the bags and grabbed the bag.

I just sat there and didn't say anything - Mauu said don't think I'm mixing poison.

He grabbed a glass of hot milk in front of me and told me to take a sip like a golden boy.

I started kissing the hot milk little by little - just like Mauo is swallowing me little by little every day. Mau sat down to dress up.

****

Chapter twentieth

Aftera while, she got dressed as a new bride - she also let me wear new dhoti-Punjabi - so I read it!

A strange thrill arose in my chest... 21-22 years of excitement filled my mind, soul-soul, I got old memories all over my body!

After a while the dream was shattered!
Mauu sat at my feet like a beggar and sat down to paint his memory in a shimmering vermilion! He put a vermilion box in front of me and said, "Look at the vermilion box that was worshiped by my mother at Kalighat on the day of Mahasthami. I have kept it for so long.
I was confused.

He said again, please Sajal - just put a pinch of vermilion in my sinthi - believe me I will never ask for anything again! Never again will your wife's demands be met! This is my dream - Fulfill Sajal!

Mauu's pitiful longing is piercing my chest like a shell, and tears are falling from his eyes.
Oh God put me to any test?

What do I do now?

As time goes by, his longing is increasing!
Get up and calm down. I stood up to my words - very face to face with me!

I said I never wanted to see you as a beggar. And where is his good fortune to make you queen?

But I was taking time because I can't get drunk playing with you easily!

Well, I haven't lost my sense of justice, have you?

All right, let your dream come true!
From Mauu's hand, I dyed his sinthi with a pinch of vermilion from that vermilion box!
A glimpse of a thousand suns on the face of Mauu.

Filled with absolute devotion, Mauu bowed his head at my feet!
I gently grabbed Mauu with both hands and hugged him happily!

The bed is wrapped in a new bedcover brought with Mauu. The pillow fence has been changed. A bunch of red roses has come out of the bag. The bed is decorated with lots of rose petals.

At once the whole house was filled with dark blue color - the hearts and minds of both of them.

Mau took the bed first -

I also went to bed and first kissed Mauu gently on the forehead.

Then - on the lips

Then - like one hundred and eight lotuses all over the body.

That's what honeymoon is all about.

Thirst in the eyes - Thirst in the chest - Thirst all over the body! Mou jumped into my chest with both hands outstretched!

Then I got lost between the two of them! Uthal-pathal- whole body, mind and soul.

Once cold is the long burning of the body and mind for twenty-five years! Water is the pride of the heart melts!

Mou is still filling my throat with caress and caress! Water droplets are shining like pearls in the corner of the eye!

I'm going to put my hand in the corner of my eye.

Don't wipe it off, it's my joy - tears.

And I have nothing to ask you Sajal! It seems that the long wait is over when you have fulfilled the wishes of so many people.

Who knows, someone loves me in such a middle age venture! You believe Sajal- I have never got so much happiness in my life! The sea of happiness has never been such.

Well Mauu we are not dreaming? Won't it all end at the end of this night?

It's a dream, it's a dream,
When the desires of the mind get overwhelmed, then everything will seem like a dream, It seems like a dream.

One more thing I will pray to you, will you give me the ball? I said if I can give it to you? Put your hand on my head and bless me if there is anything called rebirth then I will get you as my husband for life! Putting my hand on my head, I prayed to the Merciful.
This is the blessing - this time? With a sweet smile on his face, he grabbed me like a treasure of yaksha. Mou was gradually lost in my chest again to be small!

****

Chapter Twenty one

Itwas a little early in the morning. We had to leave the hotel again by ten o'clock in the morning - so we packed our bags, packed our bags and left on time.

In three and a half hours we reached near Ulberia.
I said with a heavy face - Mauu, my time has come closer.

With a smile on his face, Mauu said - why are you going down alone? Let's not do your family or come a little dhu mare - Will Lankakanda be tied or not?

In reply I said no, not Lankakanda - but faith will be broken - but you will not feel its sound or flame!

Listening to my words, Mauu said in a calm and slow voice, "No, stay wrapped in the gold of your golden family. I am happy with this. You have fulfilled the dream of my teenage mind. You have fulfilled me!"

When all the colors of life faded and Sahara took the form of desert and faced death, then you came and filled me like the life-giving river of the desert - Today Sujla Sufla is my thin mind and soul after you.

Mauu got a little closer and said - but you know Sajal wants to see your family - tell me when you have time - I will come back one day And I will fly and sit across!
 I got a little closer and said- where?
 Mou gently kissed her and said where is your heart again. The rest of the time was spent in Mauu's warm embrace.

 It was twelve o'clock when I got home. Seeing me a little confused, Ginny said, "Don't be late. Get fresh after bathing. My cooking is almost over. I have made soup pona soup with glassware. Eat it. Take a nap. You will see that your body is completely full!"

 A big teddy bear for a little girl - a lovely mirror with oysters - small and big oyster fringed tuni - a chandelier with a bubble - of course everyone bought Maui with his gate stick - a big teddy bear and lots of chocolates - the little girl is very happy to get Cadbury and the house Ginny was also very happy to get the sort of things!

 The little girl grabbed me by the throat when she saw so many things - she said with a sigh - my father is the best - all right - there is no sound of pin falling.

But a super cyclone is raging in my mind.
 I can't look straight at Ginny. The little girl's best father seems sarcastic.

 My dutiful wife is doing her duty - with endless faith!

Have I done him justice?

If the wife accidentally finds out about yesterday's incident or hears from someone - that her husband did not go to work in the office - he went to spend the honeymoon with an old lover on the beach in Digha.

Not only that.

This is not a child's play, it is called marriage according to Gandharva in Hindu scriptures - which we find patterns Of the great poet Kalidasa "Abhijnan Shakuntalam" In the text - Shakuntala Dushmanta's love story.

In fact, if a husband engages in such an illicit love affair. So will the wife's devotion, respect and faith towards that husband not disappear in an instant?

The world of gold will not be crushed?

Meanwhile, the mind is becoming restless thinking about the direction of Mauu যেন even though she has nothing but her capital, she is a beggar - He wants to live like a parasite by adopting me! But has he been able to become self-sufficient even today? Will he be able to give shelter to anyone? Maui may not have been so indulgent - I should have been careful before!

If only we didn't have to face today's crisis ...

I don't think it's right for me to fly like a kite with a latai in Mau's hand. Maybe one day Maui will intentionally tear the thread.

Mouu came to Messenger at night. Mister, there is no response that Ginny got all forgotten? Remember me too but your second half.

I will forget why Mauu's mind and body have become honeyed, its taste is still attached to my whole body, so I am chewing, it means I am reminiscing!

Is that all right? You mean, like, saltines and their ilk, eh?

She has lost her deep faith in her husband - so her husband does not bother to find out if she has gone for a long time with her old girlfriend to do water sports - she is crazy about managing the family.
Is that so?

That's why - that's why I'm most afraid of Mau - I'm cheating on a chaste wife who is devoted to her husband - she has to resort to deception day by day!

Maybe so.
But I am also tied to you without me তার Don't worry so much… Introduce me to my sister and see that I will continue to be as good as my sister… Love will be heavy - you see!
I do not know what will happen?
And yes, your boss is back?

No, he is stuck in an emergency work, he will be on the phone three days late!
But that came back so soon?

And I was in a hurry to understand? After one night, Babu fell asleep with his eyes full of thoughts.

No, that's not true.

Why would it be better to spend another night? What if all the birds eat fish and the fault of the fisherman?

Exactly so - today but so far

I understand why Ginny was summoned? How do you know?

The girls know everything, they understand everything. Good night

Happy Honeymoon.

****

What happens next?

It is gradually becoming public. The second part of "Twilight Light" is in the Volume - III Dear readers, how did "Twilight Light" feel? Don't forget to let us know. My email id. patragopal561@gmail.com